&

Arthur's Last Stand

Alan Coren

Illustrated by John Astrop

Chrysalis Children's Books
Robson Books

A Robson Book

This edition first published in the UK in 2003
by Chrysalis Children's Books,
an imprint of Chrysalis Books Group plc,
The Chrysalis Building,
Bramley Road,
London W10 6SP

All characters in this book are fictitious and any resemblance to real persons, living or dead, is purely coincidental.

British Library Cataloguing in Publication Data for this book is available from the British Library.

ISBN: 1 84458 006 7

Printed and bound in Great Britain
by Mackays of Chatham plc

The Arthur Books

* 2 great stories in one *

Arthur the Kid & Buffalo Arthur
Railroad Arthur & The Lone Arthur
Klondike Arthur & Arthur's Last Stand

Contents

Klondike Arthur

For Stefanie

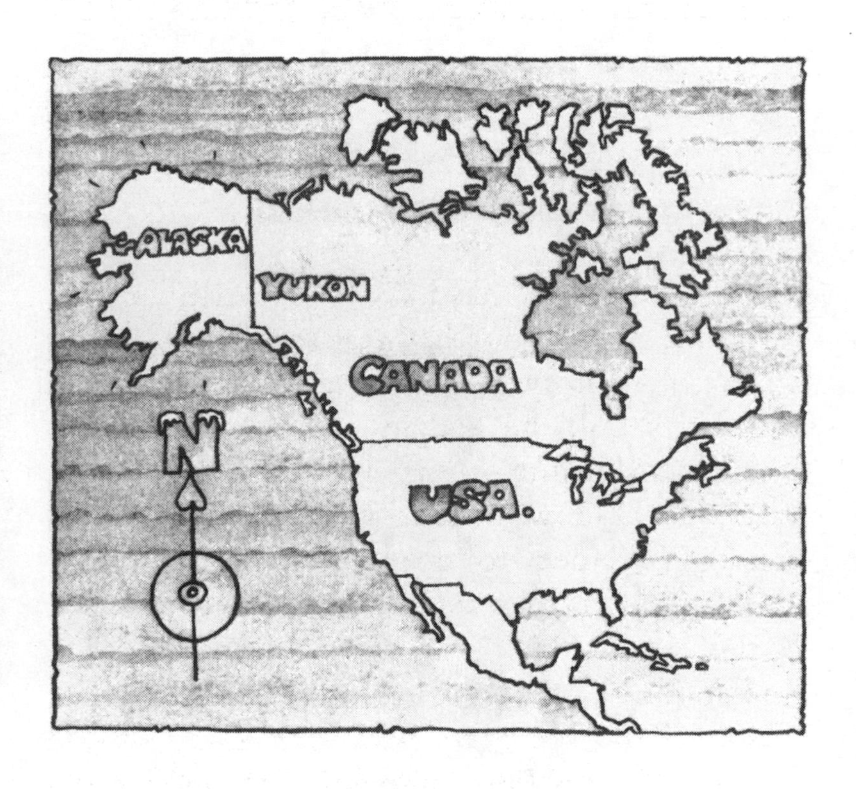

Once upon a time, a little over a hundred and fifty years ago, in the far North-West of America (so far North, in fact, that it was as close to the North Pole as it was to the United States!), a very odd deal took place.

The Russians sold Alaska to the Americans!

But if it seems somewhat strange to us today that a piece of territory more than ten times the size of England should be bought and sold, remember that it wasn't quite so strange in 1867 when this particular sale was made and when powerful countries tended to do pretty much as they liked with what they considered belonged to them by right.

It wouldn't be anything like as easy to do it today.

Especially at the price. Because Alaska was sold for only $7,200,000; and although over seven million dollars sounds, I know, like an enormous amount of money, it actually worked out at exactly one cent per acre, which is a very *tiny* amount of money. To give you some idea, at that price you could buy Trafalgar Square for tuppence!

Why on earth did the Russians let Alaska go so cheaply, is what you're probably wondering; and, do you know, that was exactly the question the Russians were asking themselves just a few years later, at about the time this story begins. Because the Russians had believed they were selling half a million square miles of ice and bare rocks and tundra and reindeer; a wasteland, in short, and a bleak and freezing and uninhabitable one, at that. What they didn't know was that in 1880 a lonely fur-trapper trying to eke out a living along the icy banks of the Yukon River would one day dig out a hole to build himself a shelter against the piercing wind.

And that he would notice, when he'd finished, something at the bottom of that hole.

Something which had once been a hidden part of the brown-black rock that surrounded it, but which time and the constant movement of underground water had gradually separated, until it lay exposed, like a dull yellow walnut. Not much to look at; but in the years that followed its discovery on that grim grey day, many thousands of men would flock to the Yukon, ready to die and, worse, ready to kill, just to get their greedy hands on it, as countless other men had done down the long centuries before them.

For it was gold!

And because it was gold, and because that one nugget meant that the Alaskan earth might be full of it, no sooner had the news broken than all over America men left their jobs, and left their wives, and left their children, and in many cases left their senses, too, and grabbed shovels and picks and, unfortunately, guns, and began to scurry north just as fast as their mules and wagons and legs could carry them. The Great Alaskan Gold-Rush had started! And for every man who hoped to make an honest strike and find his own gold, there was another who had no intention of doing any prospecting at all, but planned instead to steal the gold that others dug.

Worse, men were killed not only for their gold. So lawless, so wicked, so very, very crazy were the Gold-Rush towns, that men shot one another for their boots, for their ear-muffs, or simply for not saying "Good morning". In the saloons, waiters were shot for putting their thumbs in the soup, and barmen were shot for forgetting who ordered whiskey and who ordered beer. In the barber-shops, barbers were shot for cutting off too much hair, or too little. And as for dentists who pulled out the wrong tooth…

In short, just about the best way to get rich quickly in Alaska was to forget about digging for gold altogether and open an undertaker's business!

And just about the *second* best way to get rich quickly was to run a saloon: because after a hard day's prospecting, the one thing every miner wanted to do was come in from the terrible skin-cracking cold, into somewhere with a roaring stove and cheerful company, somewhere to buy a drink to warm the blood and bring the circulation back to frozen fingers and red noses and blue ears, somewhere with a piano, where men sang songs and told jokes and swopped stories of the day's doings among the bleak blackness of the mines and the bleak whiteness of the snow.

The piano was very important indeed. No saloon could stay in business long without a piano, and if

you think about it for a moment, I'm sure you'll understand why. Can you imagine what life would be like without music? Without songs to cheer you up when you were sad, and songs to celebrate with when you were happy? And if you can imagine how grim it was to be a miner in terrible lost Alaska, a thousand miles from anywhere, and even further from the friends and families you'd left behind, well, it's not difficult to see how much the gold-miners needed a bit of music to brighten things up. Especially as miners were roughly divided into two sorts: those who'd found gold, and those who hadn't; in other words, those who were extremely cheerful and wanted to sing, and those who were extremely miserable and wanted cheering up.

Which was why the pianist of The Rotten Old Saloon in Dogsnose Gap was such a very important man.

I think I ought perhaps to explain why The Rotten Old Saloon was called that, because it's quite possible you haven't already heard. Come to think of it, you may not even know why the town was called Dogsnose Gap.

The truth of the matter was that the Gold-Rush towns sprang up very quickly. One moment there would be nothing but a flat stretch of snow, the next it would be filled by wooden huts and loony miners rushing about digging and shooting and drinking and singing, and so on. Now, the first man to arrive in Dogsnose Gap, before, of course, it was called anything at all, was a man by the name of R B Flink. He was accompanied by his friend James Rumbold, and as they had, in fact, come from California, which is a warm and soft and sunny state, the first thing that struck them was the fearful weather.

"This place," announced R B Flink, dismounting from his mule, and slapping his frostbitten hands together, "is colder than a dog's nose!"

They stared together at the unending whiteness.

"I wonder what it's called," said James Rumbold.

"It's not called anything," replied R B Flink.

"It'll have to be called something soon," said James Rumbold.

"Then," said R B Flink, "we'll call it – hang on – Dogsnose Gap!"

And that was that.

After which more miners arrived, and builders and carpenters and gamblers and barmen and cooks and barbers and undertakers and all the rest poured in, so that in less time than it takes to tell, Dogsnose Gap was a thriving shanty town.

And of all the ramshackle buildings, with their rough-planked walls and their tarred-felt roofs and their lopsided windows and their crooked tin chimneys, the most important – apart, of course, from the undertaker's – was The Rotten Old Saloon.

Naturally, it had not been named The Rotten Old Saloon by the man who owned it: he was a rather fat, rather plum-faced, rather pompous man from San Francisco, who knew that prospectors would pay almost anything to get a drink; so that when the Alaskan Gold-Rush started, he had sped north in the hope of making his own pile of gold without actually having to dig for it, and opened a place called Hubert Tiddle's Amazing Pleasure Palace.

Named, of course, after himself, since Hubert Tiddle was as vain as he was pompous.

And he painted the wooden front of his saloon in green and gold and crimson, and he draped it with flags, and he announced A Grand Gala Opening, all to attract customers.

But he didn't spend much money on the inside, and when he threw open the doors on Gala Day and the great mob of prospectors burst through, they stopped in their tracks; because, far from being a pleasure palace, it was just a long bar and a scattering of bare wooden tables, with sawdust on the floor instead of a carpet.

"Why," cried the miners, "it's just a rotten old saloon!"

And, much to Hubert Tiddle's annoyance, the name stuck.

Still, it was the only saloon in Dogsnose Gap, and when it was full of customers, it was a pretty cheery

spot, with a great log fire crackling away at one end and, at the other, most important, a piano. And all day long, and all night, too, the old piano rocked and jangled, pouring out glad songs and sad songs, comic songs and serious songs, filling not just the saloon but also the heads and hearts of all who came to drink there with tunes and cheer. For the pianist was none other than Memory Nobbs, called that because he had not only heard more tunes than anyone else in America, that is to say one thousand, two hundred, and thirty-four, *he could also remember one thousand, two hundred, and thirty-three of them!*

Memory Nobbs was small and very thin, with long delicate fingers that had been flattened at their tips, like teaspoons, from all the long years of playing; and his face was mostly smile, because he liked nothing better than making other people feel good, and up there along the Klondike, Memory Nobbs made people feel very good indeed.

In fact, he had only one other expression besides his enormous smile, and that was a sort of mild puzzlement, a pursing of the lips, a furrowing of the brow, a very slight shake of the head. He had this expression for only about a minute or so a day, but he did have it every day, and that was because, as I think you may have guessed, it was the expression which came on when he was trying to remember the one thousand two hundred and thirty-fourth tune.

Did it go something like this? Or perhaps something like that? Did it start high up, PING? Or low down, BONG?

It was no use: try as he might, whistle though he did, and hum, and run up and down the scale, and lie awake sometimes sorting out notes in his head, Memory Nobbs just

couldn't

quite

remember

it.

But then he would shake his head, and laugh, and tell himself that it really didn't matter, and he'd start thumping away at one of the other one thousand two hundred and thirty-three, and the miners would sing and stamp their feet and forget the cold and the disappointment and the fact that their loved ones were a thousand miles away, and

The Rotten Old Saloon would rock and rattle and tinkle to Memory Nobbs and his miraculous piano.

Until, that is, that terrible night in November.

It had been one of Dogsnose Gap's better days.

Eleven prospectors had made gold strikes, which was more than usual; and this always cheered everyone up, even the most envious ones, because it meant there was plenty of gold around and if you just kept on searching and digging and panning and praying, then one day…

So The Rotten Old Saloon was even noisier than usual, with eleven prospectors celebrating and buying drinks for everyone else, including Memory Nobbs, who was therefore kept so busy in playing request numbers as a way of saying thank you that he had to play everything twice as fast as normal, just to get them all in.

He was halfway through *Dixie*, which was everybody's favourite Civil War song, and the prospectors in consequence were marching up and down the long sawdusty floor in ranks of three, shovels over their shoulders and voices making all the glasses on the bar jiggle up and down, when the door to the street flew open and the fearful Klondike gale howled through the room on a whirling shower of snow.

The miners spun round, ready to shoot whoever had been inconsiderate enough to leave the door open; but when they saw who it was, they stopped, stock-still, as if the whistling wind had suddenly frozen them where they stood.

Their singing died in their throats!

Their eyes goggled in their heads!

And the only movement in the room was that of Memory Nobbs's fingers as they flew up and down the keyboard, and the only sound above the wind was that of Memory Nobbs's tinkling notes.

For Memory Nobbs had been too absorbed in his playing to notice that the enormous thing framed in the doorway was none other than Grizzly Wilkinson!

Who was so terrible, that he was generally considered to be not only the most terrible man in Alaska, but also the second and third most terrible, too.

And if I began to list the terrible things that Grizzly Wilkinson had done, you would in all probability faint dead away; so I shall just inform you, for the record, that he had earned his strange name on one typically terrible day when a giant grizzly bear had wandered into his camp and attempted to pinch his breakfast. Whereupon Algernon Wilkinson (as he then was) walked up to the grizzly bear, knocked it flat with a single blow of his enormous fist, then sat down on it to finish his breakfast.

So you can see why no one dared tell him to shut the door. They just stood there, shivering, and not just with the cold, either.

Grizzly Wilkinson strode into the room, looking – since his giant body was covered in

a black bearskin coat and his giant face was all but covered in black beard and hair – like a grizzly himself; and his staring yellow eyes, blazing out of the black hairy mass, never left Memory Nobbs, still pounding his piano and bouncing up and down cheerily on his piano stool.

The terrible mouth of Grizzly Wilkinson opened:

"I DON'T LIKE MUSIC!" he roared.

"I wish I was in Dixie, hooray, hooray!" sang Memory Nobbs, still not looking up. "In Dixieland I'll take my stand, to live and…"

The reason he stopped was that he suddenly found himself several feet above the ground, with his little legs dangling, and his face pressed up against the terrible beard of Grizzly Wilkinson. Memory Nobbs's famous smile sort of, well, fell off. The mouth that it had just left opened and shut, but nothing came out. With one enormous hand, Grizzly Wilkinson held him clear of the ground, and with the other he tapped Memory Nobbs on the chest, ominously gently.

"When I say I don't like music," growled Grizzly Wilkinson, and though his growl was quieter than his roar it was somehow even more terrible, what I *mean* is **I don't like music**!"

Whereupon he walked slowly across to a row of pegs, hung Memory Nobbs on one of them beside the miners' coats, walked back to the piano, lifted

it above his black head without even grunting, and tossed it into a corner with no more effort than if it had been a sack of feathers.

The beautiful piano landed with one of the most heart-breaking noises it is possible to hear, a jangling mixture of BOINGS and DONGS and BANGS and TWANGS as everything inside it exploded into a thousand pieces and collapsed into a splintery heap of firewood with a last pitiful PING!

And before the horror-stricken miners had recovered from the shock (not, though, that they would have dared to do anything about it), Grizzly Wilkinson had stomped back through the room and out again into the freezing blackness, slamming the door with such force that the unfortunate Memory Nobbs was jolted from his peg and deposited upon the floor beneath.

He buried his face in his delicate hands.

"Why did he do it?" he cried.

"Because," said a miner darkly, "he is Grizzly Wilkinson."

The others nodded.

No other explanation was needed.

"There isn't another piano for a hundred miles!" cried Memory Nobbs. "And *that* one belongs to No-Nose Muldoon, who wears two guns and shoots anyone who asks him to play *Come Into The Garden, Maud.* Not the sort of man you could get a piano away from at all! It'll take six months to get another one."

The miners stared at the floor, not daring to think what life would be like without music.

Gloom descended on The Rotten Old Saloon, a thick miserable silence punctuated only by grunts and sighs and low sad mumbles as the miners grew sorrier and sorrier for themselves. And even sorrier than all his customers was Hubert Tiddle, who had enough experience about gold-rush saloons to know that unless prospecters were given some sort of entertainment to take their minds off their troubles, pretty soon they'd start making their own entertainment, which simply meant that they'd start chucking tables through his windows and shooting holes in his mirrors.

Which was almost exactly what happened, with the slight but important difference that it was through Hubert Tiddle himself that his customers decided to shoot holes!

Unable to get their own back on anyone for wrecking their piano, since they were all so terrified of Grizzly Wilkinson, they decided to put the blame on poor Hubert Tiddle; so they stood him on the table, while he wriggled and shrieked, and they nailed his boots to the table-top so he couldn't move, and they took out their revolvers, and they threw a coin to see who would get first shot, and they stood in a line waiting their turn behind the winner, and they aimed their guns, and…

And who knows what awful things might not have happened if, at that very moment, a small, yet very clear and very strong voice, had not announced, from somewhere behind them:

"I SHOULD LIKE TO RECITE A POEM ENTITLED *I'D MUCH RATHER HAVE MY MUMMY THAN ALL THE GOLD IN THE WORLD* BY ARTHUR WILLIAM FOSKETT!"

The miners paused!

The miners stared at one another!

Had their ears deceived them!

Had someone said he was going to recite a poem?

They turned, guns still out. There, on the stairs that led up to the bedrooms, stood a small boy of about seven. The miners gasped! Even Hubert Tiddle, who had put his hands over his face in terror, opened his fingers now to peep through at the interruption.

The small boy looked at them all very calmly, and cleared his throat. He did not seem in the least bit scared of these dreadful men who normally shot people who interrupted them without a second thought. And before the miners could recover from their shock enough to complain that what they wanted was a piano and not a recitation, the small boy began!

"Last night, by the Klondike River,
I dug up a fortune in gold!
But I caught a chill on my liver,
Brought on by the bitter cold!
It was far too late to push on,
So I placed the sack at my head;
But gold makes a very hard cushion,
And ice makes a very cold bed.
So I stared at the stars above me,
As my freezing body lay;
And thought of the folk who loved me,
A thousand miles away.
The voice of my dear old mother
Seemed to cry from the ice rocks:
'I told *you to wear another*
Woolly, and extra socks!'
My body is stiff. I shall die here,
In this lonely Klondike ditch;
And all I can think as I lie here,
Is: Why did I want to be rich?
There's a block of ice in my tummy,
And my frozen toes have curled.
Oh, I'd much rather have my mummy
Than all the gold in the world!"

When the small boy finished, he bowed.

There was a very long silence. Then, as one by one the miners took out their red-spotted handkerchiefs, there came the sound of sad noses

being blown, and deep sighs being sighed, and, here and there, a sob or two being sobbed. Slowly, the miners replaced their guns in their holsters; slowly, they detached Hubert Tiddle, who was also crying softly, and lowered him gently to the ground.

And then Ironface Sam McGhee, the toughest miner of all, who had six different knife scars on each cheek and a deep dent in his forehead from a shovel-fight, looked up at the small boy, and said:

"That was the most beautiful poem I have ever heard!"

And everyone agreed, nodding as they snuffled, murmuring as they wept.

"Who is this Arthur William Foskett?" asked Ironface Sam McGhee.

"I am," said the small boy.

"*WHAT*?" cried the miners.

Hubert Tiddle, recovering remarkably quickly from his fearful ordeal, rushed up and grasped Arthur's hands in his.

"Did I hear right?" he yelled. "Do you know more poems, too?"

"Oh, yes," replied Arthur. "As a matter of fact, I have written one hundred and forty-seven. They're probably not very good," he added quickly, in case anyone should think he was boasting. "I just thought it looked like the sort of moment when a poem might take people's minds off doing something pretty awful. I mean, I wouldn't normally dream of pushing myself forward like that and making people listen to me."

"Nonsense!" exclaimed Hubert Tiddle, who was recovering more rapidly every second, now that he

had spotted what looked like another golden opportunity to make money. "Why, you could make this the most famous saloon in all Alaska! There's nothing miners like more than a little light entertainment, and now we haven't got a piano any more, good heavens! – you could make all the difference to my, er, I mean, to *their* lives."

Arthur looked at him.

"What about Mr Nobbs?" he enquired.

"Oh, *him*!" said Hubert Tiddle, waving his hand airily. "You don't want to worry about him. What good's a pianist without a piano?"

"That," said Arthur firmly, "is most unfair. It isn't his fault his piano got smashed. You'll have to carry on paying him, if you want me to do recitations. You don't," continued Arthur, as he saw Hubert Tiddle's plumy face go suddenly white, "have to pay *me*. I'll do it for the fun of it."

At this, Hubert Tiddle brightened again, even though he could not possibly understand why anyone should want to do anything for nothing; but, then, that was only one of the many differences between Arthur and Hubert Tiddle. So Hubert Tiddle said, very quickly, in case Arthur should change his mind:

"Done!"

They shook hands on the deal, with Hubert Tiddle, not at all surprisingly, beaming from one

fat pink ear to the other.

"Tell you what," he said, his little eyes glowing, "we'll put up a big sign outside the saloon! THE GREAT FOSKETT: POEMS RECITED WHILE YOU WAIT!"

Arthur shook his head.

"I shouldn't like to be called The Great anything," he said. "Everybody would think I was showing off, and they'd be right. What about THE ORDINARY FOSKETT?"

"Don't be silly!" snapped Hubert Tiddle. "Who'd want to listen to anybody ordinary?"

It was at this point that Memory Nobbs strolled up, dusting the sawdust from his green velvet waistcoat. His famous smile was back, and he shook Arthur's hand warmly.

"Couldn't help overhearing," he said, "and though I says it as shouldn't, I probably know as much about show business as anyone around, and my personal opinion, based on a lifetime of experience, is that you ought to call yourself Klondike Arthur. It's got a very nice ring to it."

Arthur turned the words over in his head, thoughtfully.

"You're absolutely right, Mr Nobbs," he said. "I shall take the stage name of Klondike Arthur. But," he added sternly, looking straight into Hubert Tiddle's eyes, "not in very large letters. And you'll have to put ASSISTED BY MR MEMORY NOBBS."

"I say!" cried Memory Nobbs. "That's remarkably kind of you."

"Well," replied Arthur, "I'm only helping out until you get a new piano, after all."

"Right, then," said Memory Nobbs. "I shall make it my job to announce you, keep the audience quiet, turn over your pages, and so forth."

"Thank you," said Arthur, "but it won't be necessary to turn pages. I've got all the poems by heart."

"What!" exclaimed Memory Nobbs. "It's a good job I got my name first, else we'd have to call you Memory Foskett. I say, I've just thought of something, you don't happen to remember

a tune that sort of goes a bit like, er…"

"GIVE US A POEM!" roared a voice in the mob at the bar.

For the miners, who had cheered themselves up after Arthur's sad poem with a number of large drinks, were ready for another. A hundred bearded faces turned towards Arthur; it was like looking, he thought, at an army of hedgehogs.

"Better make it a cheerful one," hissed Hubert Tiddle. He mopped his face, suddenly remembering his narrow escape. "You know what they're like if they get too gloomy."

"Right!" barked Memory Nobbs, very professionally. He jumped on a table, and whistled sharply between his teeth, and held up his hands.

"Ladies and gentlemen," he began, "I ..."

"WHAT?" roared the miners.

"I mean, gentlemen and gentlemen," said Memory Nobbs, "I take pleasure, in company with Mr Hubert Tiddle, proprietor of this splendid establishment, in presenting for your entertainment and instruction, the greatest poet in the..." – he caught Arthur's stern eye – "...the greatest poet in Dogsnose Gap: the one, the only, the amazing – KLONDIKE ARTHUR!"

He stepped down in a thunder of cheering and stamping and clapping, and Arthur took his place on the table.

"In a lighter vein," he said, since it was a phrase he had always rather liked, though he wasn't sure why, "I should like to recite a short poem entitled *A Klondike Disaster.*"

"What?" muttered Hubert Tiddle, who was standing by Arthur's feet. "I thought you said it was going to be funny."

"It is," replied Arthur, "or, at any rate, it's

supposed to be!"

"GET ON WITH IT!" roared the miners.

Arthur squared his shoulders, and began:

"*A miner named Archibald Jolly*
Struck it rich, and went right off his trolley!
He was so mad for gold,
He neglected the cold,
And now he's the world's biggest lolly!"

It is said that as Arthur finished his poem, the shriek of laughter that came out of the hundred assembled throats echoed so far across the Alaskan night that miners at the bottom of their holes five miles away suddenly looked up, wondering if an avalanche was starting! It is said that packs of Arctic wolves, hearing the strange noise rolling towards them, began to howl themselves, throwing back their heads, and that the howls rose and fell from pack to pack, like a siren, until the laugh that began in The Rotten Old Saloon had set all Alaska going and the very polar bears, right up beyond the Arctic Circle at the North Pole itself, reared up on their hind legs in surprise and didn't sit down again for an hour!

The miners screamed! The miners choked! The miners fell on the floor, clutching their sides and rolling about until the sawdust inside was whirling

as much as the snowflakes outside! And no sooner had the laughter begun to die down into helpless gasping, then one miner would catch another's eye and cry "WORLD'S BIGGEST LOLLY!" and the whole thing would start up all over again!

Klondike Arthur looked at them.

"It wasn't *that* funny," he murmured.

Memory Nobbs wiped the tears from his eyes.

"Oh yes, it was!" he gasped. "Don't forget, we've all been out here for ages. We haven't heard any new jokes for a year!"

Slowly, the miners struggled to their feet, and called for more beer, and slapped one another on the back, and came up to Arthur, beaming and chuckling and shaking his hand. He had never seen them so happy before!

And as for Hubert Tiddle, his entire head was glowing like a great pink lantern!

"Amazing!" he cried. "Amazing!"

"Thank you very much," said Arthur. "May I go now?"

"Go?" exclaimed Hubert Tiddle. "The evening's just beginning! You said you knew a hundred and forty-seven poems."

"I do," replied Arthur, "but it's my bedtime. I go to bed at half-past seven sharp, except for Saturdays, when I stay up till eight o'clock."

"Well, *we'll* allow you to stay up as late as you like!" cried Hubert Tiddle. "This is Alaska, and anything goes!"

"I know," said Arthur, "and that's one of the things that's wrong with it. It isn't a question of allowing, Mr Tiddle. I go to bed at 7.30 because I want a good night's sleep."

"Oh, please!" wheedled Hubert Tiddle. "Just one more poem, just a little one, please stay up for just five more minutes!"

How odd, thought Arthur, to have a grown-up begging a little boy to stay up for five more

minutes, instead of the other way round! It was certainly true, as everyone said, that Alaska did strange things to people. He sighed.

"All right, Mr Tiddle, but *only* five minutes. I don't want to have you saying afterwards 'Oh just another five minutes' and all that kind of nonsense."

Hubert Tiddle nodded, and Memory Nobbs jumped up on the table again. Immediately, the miners fell silent, waiting expectantly.

"Would you care for another recitation?" asked Memory Nobbs.

"YES!" roared the miners.

Memory Nobbs frowned.

"Yes what?"

The miners dropped their eyes, and shuffled their feet.

"Yes, please," they mumbled.

"Then," cried Memory Nobbs, "by popular request, and following his recent astounding success, that versatile versifier, that pocket-sized poet, that rollicking rhymester, Klondike Arthur, returns to our stage WITH ANOTHER NEW POEM!"

Amid the whistling and cheering, Arthur climbed onto the table. He turned to Memory Nobbs.

"Funny or serious?" he asked quickly.

"Funny, I think," replied Memory Nobbs.

"You've put 'em in the mood. Another sad poem, and they wouldn't know where they were."

Arthur moistened his lips; the crowd went quiet.

"This one is another short poem," he said, "also about Alaska. It's called *An Amazing Bit Of Digging*, by Arthur William Foskett again:

"I have heard there was never a finer
Man at digging than one Klondike miner
Who started from here,
Dug straight down for a year,
And eventually came out in China!"

The audience was still crashing into the furniture and shrieking its head off when Klondike Arthur, quietly and thankfully, slipped away to bed.

Within the week, Dogsnose Gap was the most famous town in Alaska, and Klondike Arthur was its most famous citizen.

Night after night, The Rotten Old Saloon was packed not only with local prospectors but also with men who had come from many miles away to listen to the small boy whose fame had somehow spread to every gold-field and to every mining camp and to every shanty town in the territory. And not the sort of men, either, you would immediately think of as poetry-lovers; but the fact of the matter is that none of them had ever listened to poetry before, so they had always considered it cissy, and never realised that it had anything to do with real life at all.

But it is really about very real and ordinary things, as the miners found out: Arthur recited poems about being afraid and about being lonely, and about being happy and about being lucky; he had poems about the cold, and about the heat, and about food, and about animals, and about home, and about children – in short, Arthur had poems on just about every subject there was. And when he had finished one, whatever it was about, there was always somebody sitting in The Rotten Old Saloon who would nod his head and wish he'd said that,

because Arthur had managed to put into words what so many of them felt or thought.

And, do you know, their behaviour actually improved? Memory Nobbs was the first to notice that they weren't quite as rude or as angry any more, and it certainly didn't take Memory Nobbs to notice that far fewer people were getting shot; and all this may just have been because Klondike Arthur's poetry had a way of making people feel that there were more important things in life than money, and certainly that there were more important things to get shot over than a dirty look or wanting someone else's bedsocks!

In fact, sometimes, particularly when trouble looked as thought it was about to start, Arthur would quickly think up a poem on the spur of the moment, usually one of his funny ones, and everybody would laugh and put their guns away and shake hands, and the trouble would be over before it had even properly started.

For example, one night a number of miners from another town rode in on their mules, stomped into The Rotten Old Saloon, and boasted, very stupidly, that they could drink more than any man in Dogsnose Gap. Now the Dogsnose Gappers were very proud of themselves, and as silly as they were proud, so that pretty soon everyone was drinking far more than was good for them, and

Hubert Tiddle rushed into the back room where Arthur and Memory Nobbs were eating steak pie and boiled potatoes, and yelled:
"Do something quick! They're all so drunk that any minute now the shooting'll start and there'll be blood all over my nice clean sawdust!"

So Arthur and Memory Nobbs put down their knives and forks and hurried into the saloon, and Memory Nobbs whispered:
"Have you got a poem about how silly it is to get drunk, Klondike Arthur?"
And Arthur thought for a moment and said:
"No, but give me a minute, and I will have!" and began to turn rhymes over in his head frantically

while Memory Nobbs beat on the table with his shoe, so that everyone stopped arguing and looked at him, and just in time, too, since a number of pistols were glinting wickedly in the lamplight, and a number of horrible-looking knives were flashing bright darts on the ceiling.

"...proudly present Klondike Arthur!" called Memory Nobbs's voice into the sudden silence, and Arthur mounted his usual table.

"A short poem entitled *The Trouble With Drinking Too Much*," announced Klondike Arthur, "by Arthur William Foskett."

He cleared his throat.

"A drunken prospector called Bruce
Once climbed, by mistake, on a moose!
And yelled: 'This darned bike
Makes a noise I don't like,
And the handlebar's terribly loose!'"

Well, of course, the miners not only began laughing, the way they always did, they also realised, a bit sheepishly, that Arthur was getting at them, and quite right, too. So they looked at one another, and grinned, and it was all right, after that, and the drinking slowed down a bit, and Hubert Tiddle could breathe again.

But not, unfortunately, for long.

Because, on the very next night, just as The Rotten Old Saloon was settling down for the evening to a little fun and relaxation, with Klondike Arthur reciting to a packed and cheering audience, the door which had been flung open on an earlier fateful occasion was suddenly flung open again!

With the same terrible force!

By the same terrible man!

Arthur, who was halfway through one of his rather sad poems about a dog that was stuck down a rabbit-hole, stopped in mid-line. Across the length of the huge saloon, the awful eyes of Grizzly Wilkinson burned straight at him!

"GO ON!" cried the audience. For they had been so absorbed in the poem that they had not heard the door crash open, nor felt the blast of Arctic cold.

"AND," roared Grizzly Wilkinson, as though he were just adding to the last words he had spoken a month ago, "IF THERE'S ONE THING I HATE EVEN MORE THAN MUSIC, IT'S POETRY!"

One or two of the more cowardly miners fainted!

At least three screamed!

The rest just turned their heads, very slowly, praying that they had made a mistake; and, when they realised they hadn't, went very, very pale indeed.

As for Hubert Tiddle, he dropped to his knees, put his little fat hands together, and closed his eyes.

But Klondike Arthur neither screamed, nor fainted, nor prayed, nor even went the faintest shade paler. He simply stared straight back into Grizzly Wilkinson's eyes, and said quietly:

"Then I can't see why you've come. You're welcome to stay and listen, of course, but if you're going to keep interrupting like that, then I'd much rather you turned round and went out again."

As one, the miners rolled off their chairs and slid under the tables! For nobody had ever spoken to Grizzly Wilkinson like that and lived, and it could be only a matter of seconds before

Klondike Arthur was splattered all over the walls!

And indeed, Grizzly Wilkinson's huge yellow eyes were rolling like marbles in a saucer; and his furious breath whistled through his beard like a bitter gale in a dark forest, and his great hairy hands went to his guns, and his giant thumbs clicked back the hammers as the guns flashed up towards Klondike Arthur!

They stayed there for a very long second; until, suddenly, the thumbs eased the hammers down again, and the hands slid the guns back into their black holsters.

The miners, fingers in their ears, peered out from beneath the tables, not believing their eyes. And then Grizzly Wilkinson broke the dreadful silence:

"I don't think I shall shoot anybody today," he said. "Because the last thing I want is a mess all over my saloon!"

The crouching miners unstopped their ears. Surely Grizzly Wilkinson hadn't said what they thought he'd said?

Arthur, his heart still clattering despite the brave look on his face, was the first to reply.

"What do you mean, *your* saloon?" he said.

Grizzly Wilkinson reached inside his bear-skin coat, took out a large leather pouch, and tossed it onto a table.

"While some people were singing," he said, very sneeringly, "and while some people were listening to poetry, other people were digging!"

"*He's struck gold!*" whispered the miners, from the floor. "*Grizzly Wilkinson has struck gold!*"

"RIGHT!" roared the giant. "And do you know what I'm doing with my first bag of it? I'm buying this saloon, that's what!"

"Oh, *are* you?" enquired Klondike Arthur stoutly. "Mr Hubert Tiddle might just have something to say about that!"

Grizzly Wilkinson threw back his huge head and laughed. And terrible though his roar was, and even more terrible his growl, both were nothing compared with his terrible laugh!

"Oh, might he, though?" he said. He snatched up the pouch of gold again and hurled it across the room to the trembling Tiddle, who staggered with the weight as he caught it against his tummy. "I'd

like to buy your saloon, Tiddle," said Grizzly Wilkinson. He took out his guns again. "I'm offering a fair price, but, of course, if you refuse, then it obviously won't be *my* saloon, and" – here he paused, spinning his revolvers on his enormous forefingers – "I shan't mind making a mess all over it!"

Hubert Tiddle, who had gone by this time from white to pale green, nodded vigorously.

"It's yours!" he shrieked.

"Thank you," muttered Grizzly Wilkinson. "I've always wanted a saloon of my own. Nice little business, regular money coming in, *and*" – his glaring eyes swivelled about the room – "a place I could come in the evenings, a nice quiet place, without nasty music, without horrible poetry, without a lot of rowdies charging about and annoying people!"

Beneath their tables, the miners groaned to themselves; for they dared not groan out load. So that was what was to become of their lovely Rotten Old Saloon: a place without entertainment and without fun, where everyone had to walk on tiptoe and speak in whispers in case the owner got annoyed and started shooting his customers! And there was no chance that anyone would dare open another saloon across the road; not when they had Grizzly Wilkinson to compete with.

Life in Dogsnose Gap, reflected the miners wretchedly, was going to be pretty grim from now on. Not that they had much time to think about it, since Grizzly Wilkinson suddenly struck one of the tables with his pistol-butt and roared:

"COME ON! IT'S TIME EVERYBODY STARTED DRINKING! YOU'RE NOT SPENDING ANY MONEY DOWN THERE!"

And, one by one, the unhappy miners crept out from their hiding-places, stood up, and began to walk miserably towards the bar.

After that, life in Dogsnose Gap was even grimmer than they had anticipated. The gloom that descended on The Rotten Old Saloon spread through the town and the mining camps; no fresh faces travelled across the wastes to visit them, for what was there to visit? Not only were they not allowed to sing, or listen to poetry, they weren't even allowed to shout or fight or tell jokes or put mice in one another's pockets or beetles in one another's drinks, or tie one another's shoelaces together under the tables, or do any of the silly things they had always done for a laugh.

Even the joy at making a gold-strike wasn't what it had once been, since they couldn't throw parties in the saloon to celebrate; and as for the poor

prospectors who toiled all day in the freezing weather for no reward at all, imagine how they felt in the evenings, sitting in the grey grim gloom of The Rotten Old Saloon, staring at the sawdust with nothing to take their minds off their disappointments.

Especially as Grizzly Wilkinson had painted the whole place dark brown, inside and out; dark brown being his favourite colour, though (of course) nobody else's.

And then a curious thing happened; or perhaps I should say didn't happen. For it had become Grizzly Wilkinson's habit to drop into The Rotten Old Saloon every morning on his way to his mine, and every evening on his way back, just to make sure no one was laughing or singing; but one Tuesday, about three weeks after he had bought the saloon and poor Hubert Tiddle had fled back to San Francisco, Grizzly Wilkinson did not come in at all, neither in the morning, nor in the evening.

And when he didn't appear on the Wednesday morning either, the miners began to wonder.

"It'll be one of his nasty tricks," said Memory Nobbs to Klondike Arthur, as they did the washing-up in the kitchen of The Rotten Old Saloon, this being the only work for which Grizzly would pay them, and pay them precious little at that, now that they were no longer allowed to be entertainers.

"Yes," said Arthur, drying a plate very carefully. "He's probably hoping that people will think he's stopped coming in, so that they start laughing or telling jokes or something, and then he'll suddenly burst in and catch them at it."

Memory Nobbs shuddered at the idea.

"Just suppose," he murmured, "if we…"

He never finished. For at that moment there was a shout so loud, and from so many voices, that Memory Nobbs froze in terror, thinking that the strain had been too much, at last, on the customers, and now Grizzly Wilkinson would seize the opportunity he had so cunningly planned and charge in to do unimaginably terrible things to the poor wretched miners next door! He and Arthur looked at one another, horrified, then tore off their aprons to run inside and see if they couldn't stop the row before it was too late!

The scene that struck their astonished eyes was even worse than they had imagined: the shouts had turned to cheers in the space of a second, and now

the miners were rushing about the saloon and jumping up and down on the tables and throwing bottles through the windows, and rolling about on the sawdust, laughing hysterically, and doing all manner of things likely to have Grizzly Wilkinson shooting them by the dozen!

"STOP!" yelled Memory Nobbs, and when they didn't, he whistled his famous whistle, and Arthur banged a brass saucepan with an iron ladle which he had sensibly thought to snatch up as they ran in from the kitchen.

At last, the crowd fell silent, panting and grinning.

"Are you crazy?" cried Memory Nobbs. "He'll turn you into mincemeat! He'll feed you to the wolves!"

"THAT'S ALL *YOU* KNOW!" thundered Ironface Sam McGhee, the happy sweat running down the channels of his scars like raindrops on a wrinkled rock. "GRIZZLY WILKINSON IS DEAD!"

"*Dead?*" cried Klondike Arthur.

"As good as, anyway," replied Ironface Sam McGhee. "He's trapped in his mine, and he's been there for two days now. We just heard from Small Ned Chubley who rode past the Wilkinson mine this morning and saw the shaft all closed up with fallen rock. He must have dug too far in without making sure he'd propped the roof up securely, the greedy old pig, and it serves him right!"

"HURRAH!" cheered the miners.

"Wait a minute," said Klondike Arthur sharply. "Do you mean to say that he's still alive, or may be, at any rate, and here we all are doing absolutely nothing about it?"

"That's right," said Small Ned Chubley, who was only about an inch taller than Arthur, "and a good thing, too."

"But we can't just let him die!" cried Arthur.

"Whyever not?" exclaimed Ironface Sam McGhee, and all the others nodded. "Do you think

he'd risk *his* life to save any of *us*?"

"That," said Arthur firmly, "is not the point. He's more terrible than we are. If we just let him die, then we're making ourselves as terrible as he is. Don't you see?"

The miners fell silent, dropped their eyes, grew sullen, shuffled their feet, sniffed.

"Well, all right," muttered Ironface Sam McGhee. "I guess we ought to ride out and take a look."

"WURRRGH!" grumbled the miners.

"He's probably dead by now, anyhow," said Memory Nobbs, just to cheer them up; though he secretly hoped that Grizzly Wilkinson wasn't, because he felt the same way as Klondike Arthur did.

So they all climbed into their heavy outdoor clothes, and pulled on their great sealskin boots, and tugged the fur flaps of their brown beaver hats down over their ears, and trooped out onto the crunching snow, and collected their mules, and set off, out of town, towards the Wilkinson mine, with Klondike Arthur and Memory Nobbs (who didn't own mules) riding high on the buck-board of the open hearse of Thinny Skrimmerlinnet, the undertaker.

And I have to tell you, I'm afraid, that Thinny Skrimmerlinnet was actually humming to himself as he drove his two black horses, for he was

thinking that Grizzly Wilkinson's would be a very expensive funeral indeed, considering the outsize coffin he would have to have, and the fact that he was (or, hoped the undertaker, that he *had been*) a very rich man indeed, and would leave plenty of money to pay for such trimmings as brass handles and a marble tombstone, and possibly a jam tea for everyone who turned up to bury him.

And certainly, when the long winding procession finally stopped at the entrance to the Wilkinson mine, Thinny Skrimmerlinnet was absolutely certain that the funeral would take place: for where the wide black gap of the entrance had once been, with the shaft leading from it into the side of the huge snow-covered hill, there was now only a pile of great grey-black rocks, broken into enormous slabs like giant dominoes, completely blocking the way into the mine.

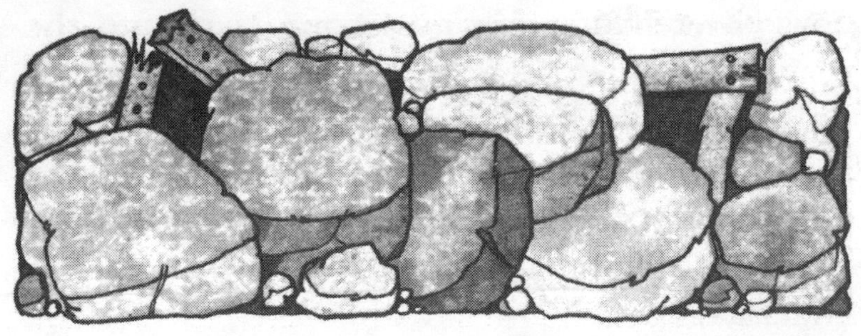

Everyone dismounted, and there were many sighs of relief puffed out on many little white clouds; but not from Klondike Arthur, who lost no time at all.

"What we need," he cried, "is a block and tackle, and ropes, and pulleys! We'll have to haul the stuff up here from Dogsnose Gap, and build it as quickly as we can, that's if he hasn't frozen to death already, and then we'll need a…"

"Hold on there!" cried Ironface Sam McGhee. "First off, we'll have to chop down trees to make the tackle, then we'll have to set up a forge right here to make the axles and the brackets, and we'll have to get a winch rigged up, and I don't know what else – some of those rocks weigh ten tons or more; all this is gonna take hours and hours; how do we know it's gonna be worth while? Even if he's still alive, by the time we get the gear working he could be dead from cold and hunger, even if he ain't got terrible injuries; I must say I don't see much point in…"

"Let's find out, then!" shouted Arthur, for he had noticed something with his extremely sharp eyes: which was that although the rocks lay piled against and on top of one another, there were here and there small gaps between, and as he clambered over them it occurred to him that there just might be a way of contacting Grizzly Wilkinson. Cupping his hands to his mouth at each of a dozen different gaps, Klondike Arthur shouted the miner's name, and once or twice that name echoed back, suggesting even wider and deeper spaces beyond.

“Does he answer?” called Memory Nobbs, watching from below. “Can you hear anything?”

Arthur shook his head.

“HURRAH!” cried the crowd, in somewhat wicked relief, while Thinny Skrimmerlinnet rubbed his hands and began to make expensive calculations with a sharp stick in the snow. “Let’s go home!”

“No!” shouted Arthur. “If we could get to him, take him a hot drink, or food, or blankets, tell him that help was coming, we might still be able to save him!”

“*Get to him?*” cried Ironface Sam McGhee. “Nobody could get through those cracks, unless he was a snake or something!”

Or a small, rather thin boy, thought Klondike Arthur. For while it was certainly true that no grown man, not even Small Ned Chubley (who made up in fatness what he lacked in height), could squeeze between the mighty slabs, there was a very slight chance that Arthur might manage it, and while a chance did exist, however slight, Klondike Arthur was not the boy to give it up. So he slid and climbed and scrabbled down the rock-pile again, and grabbed a couple of pack-blankets from the nearest mule, and asked Ironface Sam McGhee for the bottle of whiskey he always carried, and turned back once more to the ruined mine.

"You're crazy!" cried a number of miners from different parts of the crowd.

"No, he's not," murmured Memory Nobbs, as he watched Arthur begin his climb, "he's just remarkably brave."

It was true. For who could tell that Klondike Arthur would not wriggle inside the first layer of rock, and even the second, only to get trapped inside the third, where no grown-up could reach him, or crushed by a sudden movement of the fearful rocks? And indeed, as he wormed and squirmed now, barking his shins and tearing his hands and bruising his whole body (for even the thick winter clothes were no protection against the razor-edges of broken rock), Arthur felt for the first time a cold fear strike through him. For it was black, utterly black, now, in the heart of the rock maze, and he could hear the grisly grinding as the rocks settled, and he suddenly realised that he had no room to turn round, so that he could not go

back, could not get out, but only wriggle and twist and scrape his way forward, pushing the blankets before him, praying that each time a fresh layer of apparently solid rock appeared he would somehow find a large enough gap to drag his aching body through.

And, amazingly, he did!

Until, suddenly pushing between two huge boulders like twenty-ton buns, he found himself falling, turning in the air, and landing with a thump upon, luckily, the roll of blankets which had dropped beneath him.

He could see nothing. But he could hear something.

Breathing!

Klondike Arthur crawled towards the sound, and suddenly recoiled as his hand touched some unseen hairy animal with huge teeth!

Shuddering, he lit a candle. And found that what he had touched had been the huge bearded face of Grizzly Wilkinson!

Who stirred now, and groaned, but rolled over and would not open his eyes.

"I am going to die," he croaked, in the faintest of whispers.

"Nonsense!" cried Klondike Arthur sternly, and grasping Grizzly Wilkinson's hair in both hands he pulled him up into a sitting position, and uncorked the whiskey, and shoved the bottle-neck deep into the man's mouth between his blue and frozen lips.

First, Grizzly Wilkinson spluttered; then he coughed; then he drank; then he guzzled! He opened his eyes. He stared at Arthur.

"*You!*" he gasped. "Why would *you* come to rescue *me?*"

"Don't talk!" snapped Arthur. "Save your strength, help is on the way; they're building a block and tackle to lift the rocks off, but it'll take a few hours, and we've got to keep you warm."

And so saying, he wrapped Grizzly Wilkinson in the blankets, and made him drink more of the warming whiskey, and even – and just imagine it! – snuggled up against him so that some of his warmth would help take the chill off Grizzly Wilkinson's shivering body. And gradually, as he began to think that he might not die after all, Grizzly Wilkinson gazed at Arthur with those huge yellow eyes of his which shone like a lion's in the flickering light of Arthur's candle, and he murmured quietly:

"Nobody has ever done anything like this for me in my entire life before."

Which, thought Arthur, probably went a long way towards explaining things about Grizzly Wilkinson. But what he said was: "It's hardly surprising, considering the way you treat people!"

But instead of losing his temper, Grizzly Wilkinson just nodded.

"You're right," he said, "you're absolutely right."

And then, do you know, Grizzly Wilkinson, the most terrible man in all Alaska, began to cry.

"Oh, come on!" cried Klondike Arthur. "If we get sorry for ourselves, we're done for. Tell you what, let's sing a song to cheer ourselves up."

But Grizzly Wilkinson merely sniffed, and shook his head.

"I can never remember words," he said, "that's why I don't like music. I always get one song mixed up with another."

"My goodness!" cried Klondike Arthur. "I know a poem about someone just like you." And before Grizzly Wilkinson could remind him that he didn't like poetry either, Arthur began:

"There once was a miner called Bing
Who, when anyone asked him to sing,
    Replied, 'Ain't it odd?
    I can never tell God
Save the Weasel *from* Pop Goes The King*!'"*

Well, for perhaps the first time in his life, Grizzly Wilkinson produced a laugh that was not only not terrible at all, it was really rather wonderful, a great booming chuckle that re-echoed through the cave, and made Arthur laugh, too, even though he'd recited the poem a hundred times.

"Was *that* poetry?" gasped Grizzly Wilkinson, when he had finally finished laughing. "I never realised poetry could be such fun!"

"Well, then," said Klondike Arthur, "perhaps we ought to try singing, too."

So they did.

When the block and tackle shifted the last enormous rock some six hours later and the white afternoon light flooded into the shaft, the mob of rescuers could not believe their eyes, nor their ears!

Klondike Arthur and Grizzly Wilkinson were sitting side by side with their backs to the wall, singing *Polly Wolly Doodle*!

And, before the rescuers had recovered from the shock, there was another, for Grizzly Wilkinson,

his huge strength almost fully returned, leapt to his feet and began to shake their hands, and clap their backs, and hug them, throwing his enormous arms around four of them at a time!

And they all rode back to Dogsnose Gap, singing as they went. With the one exception, I'm afraid, of Thinny Skrimmerlinnet.

And as soon as they reached The Rotten Old Saloon, Grizzly Wilkinson announced that everyone could drink as much as he liked absolutely free, to celebrate the fact that he was going to repaint the place in yellow and white, *and put in a carpet*!

So they drank and laughed and drank some more, and Klondike Arthur recited eleven different poems and allowed himself to stay up until nine o'clock, and everybody had such a wonderful time that none of them noticed that, late in the evening and after Arthur had gone at last to bed, Grizzly Wilkinson had once more disappeared.

He was gone for three days; and this time the miners were really worried, for they were generally agreed that the new Grizzly Wilkinson was a very fine fellow indeed, so much so that search parties went out to look for him day and night, but with no success.

Until suddenly, at around lunchtime on the third day, and just when the miners were plunging back

into the despair from which they had so recently been rescued, the doors of The Rotten Old Saloon opened, and Grizzly himself burst in. And, so different from the last time he had done any door-bursting, this time his face was lit by an enormous smile as his mighty arms dragged something into the room behind him from his sled. The thing was

covered in a sheet, but not for long; for, as the miners gazed, Grizzly Wilkinson snatched the sheet away, and there in the middle of the newly-carpeted floor was the finest piano they had ever seen!

"Good heavens!" cried Memory Nobbs. "I'd know that piano anywhere! It belongs to No-Nose Muldoon!"

"Not any more it doesn't" replied Grizzly Wilkinson.

Klondike Arthur gave him a specially stern look.

"You don't mean," he said, "that you – "

"I know what you're thinking," said Grizzly Wilkinson, "but you're wrong. I paid for it with good yellow gold."

"A piano again!" shouted Memory Nobbs, sitting down at it immediately and running his fingers lovingly along the keys.

"Thank heavens!" exclaimed Arthur. "I had just recited my 147th poem. I was beginning to wonder what to do next."

And he was so relieved to have that particular weight off his mind that he began to whistle.

Which made Memory Nobbs fall clean off his stool!

"THAT TUNE YOU'RE WHISTLING!" he yelled. "THAT'S *IT*!"

"You mean," said Klondike Arthur, "the one you can never remember? Number one thousand two

hundred and thirty-four?"

"YES!"

"Are you sure?"

"OF COURSE I'M SURE!" cried Memory Nobbs, jumping up and down impatiently. "For heaven's sake, *tell me what it's called*!"

Grizzly Wilkinson suddenly beamed his proudest grin.

"Everybody knows that!" he roared. "It's called *Pop Goes The Weasel*!"

And he gave Klondike Arthur a very special wink.

Arthur's Last Stand

For Tobias, Jemima and Joshua

Once upon a time, about a hundred and fifty years ago, in the very middle of what is now the state of Montana but then was called Montana Territory, stood a fort.

The fort was surrounded by mountains. Indeed, there was very little in Montana that was not surrounded by mountains; which, as you've probably guessed, was why it was called Montana. For not only did the great Rocky Mountains range run right through the centre of the territory, but more than a dozen other smaller ranges criss-crossed and wandered and sprouted there, all of them with wonderful names, like the Crazy Mountains, and the Flathead Mountains, and the Bitter Root Range, and the White Fish Range, and both the Little Belt Mountains *and* the Big Belt Mountains. And within these great saw-toothed, snow-crowned ranges, individual mountains, too, had (and still have) marvellous names of their own.

So that if you want to see exactly where this particular fort stood, look on a map of the United States, find Montana, which is right at the very north and borders Canada, and look for a mountain called Bear Paw Mountain.

For Bear Paw Mountain rose up behind the fort. And in front of the fort ran Milk River, and across Milk River, on the Canadian border, rose the mountain called Old Man On His Back Plateau, which the sentry posted on the highest look-out point of the fort could just see through his telescope.

There was always a sentry up there, of course, and his telescope was always out, and the sharp mountain sun would always wink off its bright brass bands, because it was a very clean telescope indeed.

It was that sort of fort. Or, more to the point, it had that sort of commanding officer in charge of it; and whatever else people might have said about Major Oliver Spoongurgle, they had to admit that Fort Moccasin was the smartest, cleanest garrison in the entire US Cavalry.

And people *did* say other things about him, especially his men; which was hardly surprising, for Major Oliver Spoongurgle kept them hard at it, day and night, painting and polishing and cleaning. The high wooden walls of the fort gleamed the rich brown gleam of fine furniture; the

gravel of its inner courtyard was rolled and swept into stripes until it resembled a yellow lawn; and on that gravel, the neat mounds of cannonballs which stood beside the sparkling guns might have been made of gold, not iron, for all the care that had gone into making them shine.

As for the horses in the fresh-painted stables, they would have looked more at home in a circus than in an army: their manes were plaited and set off with yellow-and-blue bows (to match the men's uniforms), yellow-and-gold braid trimmed their tails, and every strap and buckle was decorated with the kind of twinkling ornament that would, no doubt, have done very well had they been pulling a royal coach, but had very little place on a battlefield.

And the cavalrymen themselves spent more time in shining their boots than in sharpening their swords, and more time in polishing their buttons than in practising with their rifles, and more time in fancy marching than in battle-training. So that it was quite understandable that from time to time the men would pause in their polishing or their sewing or their ironing to wonder just why it was that their commanding officer was so crazy about smartness; and the only conclusion they ever came to was that it must have been something to do with his name, because if you were called

Oliver Spoongurgle, they argued, you had to do everything just a little bit better than if you were called, say, John Smith, since people, being the way they are, don't need much of an excuse to start poking fun at someone called Spoongurgle.

What the men didn't know, however, and what worried them more than anything, was whether the Major was any good at fighting. For that was why Fort Moccasin had been built, after all, and that was why the cavalry was manning it.

Because these were pretty grim days in Montana. Just a year or so earlier, the Sioux, who were

probably the bravest and the toughest of all the Indian tribes, had won their greatest victory over the United States Army: a few hundred miles away, at the Little Bighorn, the Sioux had wiped out five companies of the crack 7th Cavalry, including their General, George Armstrong Custer. And afterwards, though expedition after expedition was mounted by the army, though battle after battle was fought, they never succeeded in capturing Sitting Bull, chief of the Sioux.

Even worse, from the army's point of view, was that the warriors of many other tribes – the Hunkpapa and the Oglala, the Miniconjou and the Blackfoot – had joined forces with Sitting Bull; and under their great fighting chiefs, men like Black Moon, No Neck, Iron Dog, Big Road, and Spotted Eagle, they rode out time after time to raid the forts and the villages and the wagon-trains of Montana and Idaho and Dakota.

Which was why, at the end of the 1870s, so many new forts had been hurriedly built, strung out across these states; but with so many new forts, the US Army was stretched very thin, so that few of the forts held more than a hundred men. And as the Indian raiding parties often contained up to a thousand fine riders who were not only crack shots but also clever tacticians who could plan and fight a battle as well as their blue-coated cavalry enemies, it isn't difficult to understand why Major Oliver Spoongurgle's men sometimes felt a worried shiver pass through them when they saw him holding meetings with his junior officers to discuss new curtains, when he ought, perhaps, to have been working out battle tactics!

And of all the men, none worried more about what might happen when the Indians attacked than the cook-house detail – that's to say, the three men who had to do all the dirty jobs around the fort kitchen; and these were Private Bingle, who peeled potatoes, Private Conk, who washed up, and Private Wibbley, who swept. They had not, of course, joined the cavalry in order to muck about in the kitchens, but that, unfortunately, was all that Major Oliver Spoongurgle would allow them to do.

This was not because they would have made bad soldiers, or bad horsemen, or bad shots – they never

had the chance to find out, since the Major would never allow them near guns or horses – but simply because of their shapes. For Private Bingle was a head shorter than all the other men, and Private Conk was a head taller than all the other men – except, of course, that he was two heads taller than Private Bingle – and as for Private Wibbley, he was fatter than any other three soldiers put together.

So that on the day when he took command of his company, and lined them all up before him, Major Oliver Spoongurgle had taken one look at these three odd shapes who were completely spoiling the nice neat look of the line of men, and almost fainted from the shock!

"Uggh!" he shrieked, in a somewhat un-officer-like manner. "Who are those horrible, horrible men?"

"Troopers Bingle, Conk, and Wibbley, sir," replied the sergeant beside him.

"Troopers?" exclaimed Major Oliver Spoongurgle, dabbing at his face with his lavender-scented hankie. "Troopers? I'm not having them trooping with me, they're ruining the whole look of the column, I'd just as soon have three pigs put in uniforms and following me about! This is going to be the smartest company in the entire United States Cavalry, it's going to win all sorts of prizes;

I'm not going to have it turned into a laughing-stock by those three freaks. You're not to call them troopers, Sergeant, you're not, you're *not*, you're NOT!"

The Sergeant looked at him for a bit, since he had never seen a major stamping his feet and jumping up and down before; but, of course, he did not say anything except:

"Yes, sir, very good, sir. May I refer to them as privates, sir?"

The Major sighed, and sniffed, and brushed a tiny speck of dust from his immaculate new uniform.

"Very well, if you must, you must. Personally, I go all hot and cold just thinking about them as soldiers at all. But keep them out of my sight, do you understand? If I see them again in my lovely fort, I shall probably scream."

After which Major Oliver Spoongurgle dismissed the men, and went inside with his three junior officers to choose wallpaper. Leaving poor Bingle, Conk and Wibbley to receive the wretched news that they were assigned to the kitchen forever, in order that their commanding officer might never set eyes on them again.

So you can quite understand, I'm sure, why it was that they were more worried than anyone about Indian attacks: they were allowed no guns with

which to defend themselves, no horses on which they might escape, not even a sword. All that they had to fight with was a number of large potatoes which Bingle had managed to hide and which they planned to throw at any Indians who got close enough, and three of Wibbley's broom-handles to which they had tied three of the forks that Conk had borrowed from the washing-up bowl one day, to use as spears.

Not that they had much confidence in them.

"You don't often hear," said Conk gloomily, when they'd finished the tying-on, "of wars being won by the side with the biggest potatoes."

"I don't remember hearing about The Charge Of The Fork Brigade, either," said Bingle.

"Personally," said Wibbley, "if the Indians attack, I shall chuck a bottle of tomato ketchup over my head and stick a couple of chicken feathers in my

hair. Maybe they'll never notice."

Whereupon the three friends fell silent, thinking a number of terrifying thoughts and wondering how soon it would be before the thoughts turned into something worse.

They did not have long to wait.

Three days later, on an early April morning, as the clear air began to soften with Spring, Chief Sitting Bull came across the Canadian border from the camp in which he had been planning this new campaign, and, at the head of fifteen hundred warriors, struck at villages along the Little Missouri River which wound along the Montana-Dakota border, just two hundred miles east of Fort Moccasin.

All the forts in the area were put on immediate alert, and the battle-plans of all the commanding officers swung into action. Except for those of Major Oliver Spoongurgle, who didn't have any.

He was in his new four-poster bed, admiring the colour-scheme he had chosen for his room, when his second-in-command, Captain Sam Sutton, burst in.

Major Oliver Spoongurgle sat up in bed excitedly. "The goat!" he cried. "Has it arrived?"

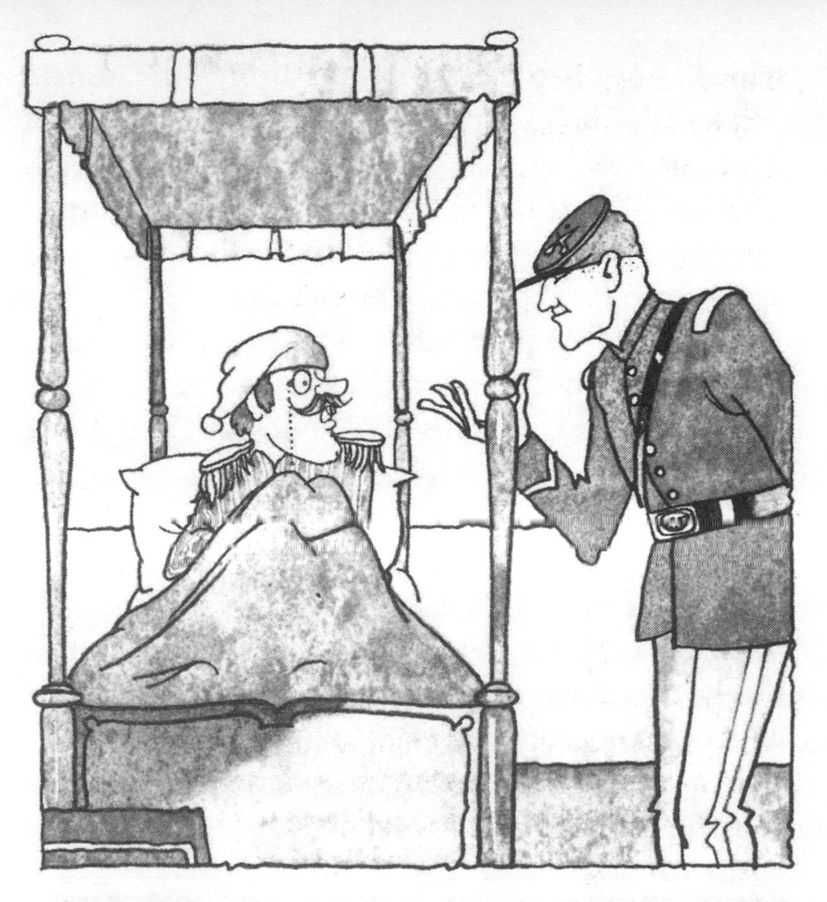

"What?" said Captain Sam Sutton, taken by surprise.

"Our new regimental goat," snapped the Major impatiently. "Our mascot! The finishing touch to my beautiful fort. The one thing every smart cavalry company must have, a big, beautiful white goat, with lovely long curly horns, a goat to lead our processions when we ride out to..."

"It's no time to talk of goats, sir!" interrupted the Captain. "Sitting Bull is on the war-path, he's

wiped out two settlements along the Little Missouri! Shall I muster the men while you dress, sir?"

"*What*?" shrieked Major Oliver Spoongurgle. "Are you mad? Are you asking me to ride out against the Poo without a proper mascot?"

"The *who*?" enquired the Captain, staring at him.

"Not the Who," rapped the Major, "the Poo!"

The Captain closed his eyes in despair, and shook his head.

"I think you mean the *Sioux*, sir," he murmured, "don't you?"

"Poo, Who, Sioux, what difference does it make?" barked the Major angrily. "The important thing is the goat. I have no intention of leaving this fort and marching anywhere until my goat arrives. I sent away for him two weeks ago, and until he turns up, we shall carry on as before."

"But, sir…"

"I rather thought," said Major Oliver Spoongurgle, sinking back against his yellow-and-blue silk pillows, "that we'd dress him in a blue horse-blanket with his name picked out in yellow embroidery. What do you say to that, Sutton?"

But the Captain had already left.

And, I'm afraid to say, without even bothering to salute.

For the next two days, while Sitting Bull's braves rampaged along the Little Missouri, skirmishing with settlers, raiding villages in lightning strikes, avoiding the pursuing cavalry companies despatched from the various forts and garrisons, and generally growing more and more daring as they grew more and more successful in their attacks, the men of Fort Moccasin waited and sweated and prayed for orders and bit their nails. None of which made the slightest impression on their commanding officer; except, naturally, for the last-mentioned.

"Bitten nails!" he yelled one morning, at early parade. "I never dreamed a company of mine should come to this! It's terrible, it's disgusting, it's so *ugly!*"

For every morning, on parade, Major Oliver Spoongurgle would inspect his command minutely: not to see whether their weapons were in working order, of course, since that was the last thing he cared about. But to see whether they had washed behind their ears, and trimmed their moustaches, and combed their hair, and put lavender-water on after they had shaved, and all that sort of thing; and when he spotted the bitten

nails, his face went so purple that, from the distance, it looked as though the fort was being commanded by a giant plum.

What particular horrible punishment he might have inflicted on them for biting their nails, however, we shall never know; for just as that moment, the sentry posted on high lookout called "PARTY APPROACHING, NORTH-EAST QUARTER" and, while the men began to shake where they stood, sure that they were about to be fallen on by the full force of Chief Sitting Bull and knowing that Major Oliver Spoongurgle did not have the faintest idea of how to defend them, Captain Sam Sutton sprang up the ladder to the ramparts, field-glasses to his eyes.

"What is it, Captain?" cried the Major nervously.

Slowly, the Captain lowered his field-glasses.

"Open wagon approaching, sir," he replied. He cleared his throat. "It appears to have a goat in it."

The soldiers gasped with relief!

And Major Oliver Spoongurgle jumped in the air and clapped his neat white-gloved hands together!

"My goat!" he cried. "My goat's arrived! Bugler, sound *Open Gates!*"

At which command the company bugler, delighted that he wasn't having to sound *Charge!* or *Man The Ramparts!* or *Watch Out for Indians!* or *Help!*, blew a few high, sweet, brassy notes, and the

man on the gate threw up the heavy wooden bar and swung open the two huge doors.

And through the doorway, a minute or so later, as the company presented arms and Major Oliver Spoongurgle raised his beautifully polished sword in salute, trundled a plain wooden wagon pulled by a rather scruffy brown mule.

In the back of this cart stood a somewhat mangy grey goat, chewing with a slow, reflective action that made its straggly little beard waggle from side to side, and idly flicking its scruffy hindquarters with what looked like a piece of old grey string but was in fact the best it could do in the way of a tail.

And on the seat in front of it, holding the reins of the elderly mule, was a small boy of about seven.

Very, very slowly, Major Oliver Spoongurgle lowered his sword until its point touched the ground. His face, so recently plum-coloured, now faded to the colour of cream cheese. His mouth, beneath the immaculate black moustache-points, fell open. Until at last, and not without great difficulty, he managed to force some words between his stricken lips.

"What," he croaked, "*is that*?"

The small boy jumped down from the seat.

"Good morning, Major," he said. "My name is Arthur William Foskett. May I introduce Webster?"

"Webster?" echoed the Major faintly.

"The goat," explained Arthur.

Major Oliver Spoongurgle swayed, as if about to faint, and put out a hand towards Captain Sam Sutton for support.

"Goat?" he murmured. "You call that thing, that mouldy flea-bag, that heap of smelly knitting – you call *that* a goat?"

Arthur looked up at the Major, slowly. When he spoke, he spoke very carefully and very politely, but very firmly.

"Webster," he said, "is not only a goat, he is probably the most intelligent goat in the world. He is also an extremely nice goat. He is not a thing, he is not mouldy, and he does not have fleas. He may smell a bit different from people" – and here Arthur paused, and sniffed deeply – "because goats do not, as far as I know, use lavender-water, but it is a perfectly proper smell for a goat."

Major Oliver Spoongurgle's face clenched like a fist.

"When I asked for a goat," he said, "I expected something white and beautiful, something smart and dignified, something behind which this elegant company would be proud to march. I also expected it to arrive properly accompanied by a troop of horse, and an officer bearing its pedigree, so that we would know that it was a goat from a good family. Who are you, and where did you get that pile of horribleness?"

Now Arthur had been brought up to treat everyone he met with respect and politeness; he also recognized that the Major *was* a major, even though, on first appearances, he didn't seem to be much of one. So he swallowed any sharp reply he

might have made to this further insult concerning Webster, and said, quietly:

"As you know, sir, there is a war on at the moment. When your request came for a regimental goat, everyone at regimental headquarters in Fort Peck was a bit busy organizing troop movements and moving cannon and working out battle tactics and all the rest of it, and I'm afraid no one had time to sort out a particular goat. In fact, you probably wouldn't have got a goat at all, except that I happened to hear about it, and I thought I ought to do my bit to help out; and as I've known Webster for a long time and know him to be a remarkably nice and intelligent goat, I decided to bring him to you."

It was Captain Sam Sutton's turn to gasp!

"Just a minute, young Arthur!" he exclaimed. "Do you mean to say you've come a hundred miles from Fort Peck *all on your own*?"

"That's right, sir," replied Arthur.

"*Through Indian country*?"

"Yes," said Arthur. "It took me five days, or rather nights, which is rather a long time, I know, but I thought it best to travel by dark. The Sioux don't attack at night, you know."

"Yes, I did know," said Captain Sam Sutton, looking at Arthur with considerable respect. "You're a very brave young man. Thank you very

much for Webster, our company will be proud to have him."

"Rubbish!" snapped Major Oliver Spoongurgle. "Nothing of the kind! I'd rather march behind a regimental rat than that thing!"

"But Major," protested the Captain, "after Arthur has brought him all this..."

"NOT ANOTHER WORD!" shouted the Major. "And if you wouldn't mind dismissing the men, Sergeant, I really must go and have a bit of a lie down. This has all been a great shock to me, you know."

Whereupon Major Oliver Spoongurgle turned on his elegant heel and marched delicately away towards his quarters, dabbing his hankie to his forehead as he went.

The men were dismissed, and went back miserably to their polishing and Captain Sam Sutton put a friendly hand on Arthur's shoulder.

"Sorry about that, Arthur," he said. "I'm afraid the Major has rather a lot on his mind at present. You'd better go round to the cook-house and get some breakfast while we work out what's best for you to do. You'll have to stay, of course; we can't possibly let you go back to Fort Peck with Sitting Bull liable to swoop down any second."

"I'll take Webster with me if I may, sir," said

Arthur, dropping the buck-board of the cart, and leading the goat onto the parade ground, "he gets pretty hungry, too."

"Of course," replied the Captain, "and I'll see to it your mule gets fed and quartered with the horses. You'll find the cock-house round the..."

But Webster, who had been sniffing the air very carefully, was already tugging on his lead and scratching at the gravel with his front hoof.

"It's all right, sir," said Arthur, "Webster will find it. He's got a very good nose for things like breakfast."

And, with Arthur nearly overbalancing at Webster's eager tug, the small boy and the goat set off at a trot towards the delicious smell of frying that was issuing in wispy puffs from the tin smoke-stack of the kitchen.

It says much for tiny Private Bingle's presence of mind that he did not faint when Webster's nose

suddenly appeared in his lap. He was sitting on the cook-house step, staring at the two hundredth potato he had peeled that morning, when the goat's scruffy muzzle shoved itself onto his knee.

"My goodness!" cried Private Bingle, dropping his peeler. "What's this, then?"

"It's Webster," said Arthur. "Potato peelings are just about his favourite food."

"What a stroke of luck!" exclaimed Private Bingle. "I was just that moment thinking I ought to gather them all up and take them round to the dustbins. Not the nicest job, I don't mind saying."

"Oh, Webster will get rid of them for you," said Arthur, "won't you, Webster?"

At which Webster, who had extraordinarily good manners and had been waiting patiently for a proper invitation, plunged his face into the enormous pile of peelings, and began to chomp.

Arthur and Private Bingle introduced themselves, and Arthur explained about the arrival of Webster and Major Oliver Spoongurgle's reaction, and Private Bingle nodded gloomily and explained, in his turn, about Major Oliver Spoongurgle.

"It doesn't surprise me," said Arthur, when he'd finished. "I should imagine *we'll* be confined to the cook-house as well."

"No doubt about it, I'm afraid," replied Private Bingle. "You're even shorter than I am, so he'll never let you near the parade ground, and you know what he thinks about Webster. Still," he went on, brightening, "it's nice and peaceful round here, the food's all right, and nobody bothers us. Come and meet the others."

So, leaving Webster with the pile of peelings (which was going down with amazing speed), Arthur followed Private Bingle into the cook-house, and shook hands with Private Conk and Private Wibbley, and sat down to a huge steaming plate of fried eggs and hash-brown potatoes and fresh sweet-corn, and pretty soon forgot his disappointment that Webster's career as a cavalry goat seemed to have ended before it had begun.

"I suppose," said Private Conk, as Arthur pushed back his empty plate, "we could always *paint* Webster white, and make a false tail out of a nice piece of rope, and cut his beard off."

"Yes, and while we're at it," snapped Private Wibbley, glaring up at him, "we could chop your legs off at the knee and glue them onto Bingle's feet, so that you'd both be the same height as everybody else! Just suit old Spoongurgle, that would."

"He's right," said Bingle. "Webster's perfectly okay as he is, he'd make an extremely good regimental mascot; it's rotten old Spoongurgle who's wrong."

"He can walk on his hind legs," said Arthur.

"Spoongurgle?" enquired Conk, puzzled.

They all stared at him.

"You'll have to forgive Conk," said Private Bingle to Arthur. "It's all on account of his being so tall. It takes ideas twice as long to get up to his brain. It's *Webster* who can walk on his hind legs," he shouted up at Conk, "you great gumboil!"

"Oh," murmured Conk.

"Yes," said Arthur. "I've trained him. It's a hobby of mine. I used to do shows with him at Fort Peck. I used to do card tricks and juggling, and Webster used to walk around on his hind legs."

"Card tricks?" cried Wibbley, clapping his podgy hands. "Juggling?"

In answer, Arthur took four soup-dishes from the drying-rack and, as Private Conk trembled (having a fair idea of what Major Oliver Spoongurgle would do it he heard that one of his precious bone-china plates had broken), tossed them in the air so fast that they seemed to turn before the Private's amazed eyes into a shimmering white cartwheel!

"I can see you're going to brighten the place up no end," said Private Bingle, as Arthur replaced the plates in their rack, to the enormous relief of Private Conk. "What else can you do, Arthur?"

"Oh, nothing much," replied Arthur, who hated the idea that he might sound boastful, while at the same time wanting to tell the truth. "I can walk on my hands a bit, and do a little ventriloquism, but that's about all."

"What on earth," asked Private Conk, "is ventle, ventro, er..."

"Ventriloquism," explained Arthur, "is the method of throwing your voice while at the same time not moving your lips..."

"...so that it looks as if the stove is speaking," said the stove.

The Privates gasped!

The Privates reeled!

"The stove," shrieked Private Conk, "it spoke!"

"Oh, shut up, Conk!" snapped Bingle.

"Shut up, Conk!" snapped the stove.

"That," cried Private Wibbley, "is the most astounding thing I ever heard, Arthur."

"Oh," murmured Arthur, "it's only a trick, it's easy when you know how. It's not nearly as difficult as..."

But what ventriloquism was not as difficult as had to remain a mystery; for at that moment, the bugler blared *Open Gates!* again, and a split second later the four friends heard the clatter of frantic hooves echo around the parade ground, and they sprang through the cook-house door, past Webster the goat (who was lying in the sun, full of food, blinking happily, and certainly in no mood to go

charging round like a mad human), and up to the wooden rails that separated the cook-house block from the square.

The soldier who leapt from the sweat-glistening horse hurled himself towards Captain Sam Sutton, who had simultaneously run to meet him, thrust a dispatch-case into the officer's hand, and began gesturing excitedly in the direction from which he had come.

The Captain tore open the dispatch case, glanced at the papers inside, turned, sprinted up the steps towards Major Oliver Spoongurgle's quarters, and disappeared inside.

"I wonder," said Arthur, "what all that was about."

What it was about, Captain Sam Sutton was at that moment making very plain to Major Oliver Spoongurgle.

"The General's orders are very clear, sir," he said. "The settlement at Beaver Creek has been overrun, and our company is to proceed there immediately and attempt to engage the enemy. May I sound the general alert?"

"Fighting!" muttered the Major, who had gone very white. "Fighting, that's all this army ever thinks about! We'll get *filthy*!"

"What?" gasped Captain Sam Sutton.

"Our uniforms, you idiot!" cried the Major. "They could get ruined! We shall probably have to fire some of our beautiful cannonballs, we may even, heaven help us" – and here he shuddered – "get blood on our swords, if we're not very careful. And may I remind you, Captain, that we do not even have a proper goat? If you think I'm taking that revolting Webster thing with us, you've got another think coming! I shan't go!"

The Captain stared at his commanding officer, and licked dry lips.

"Major, I don't think, you understand. These are *orders*! You have no alternative."

Gloomily, Major Oliver Spoongurgle stared at the dispatches. All that polishing going to waste! No goat! And, far worse, there was a good chance they'd run into the enemy, unless he could find a way of avoiding it. *This*, thought the Major miserably, was definitely not why he had joined the army. This had nothing to do with strutting about in lovely shiny boots and riding through a town on

a big white horse while people took their hats off and cheered.

But there was nothing he could do about it. Orders were orders.

Major Oliver Spoongurgle sighed heavily.

"Oh, very well," he muttered.

So Captain Sam Sutton saluted hurriedly and left, and gave his orders to the junior officers, and within a very few minutes the bugler had sounded *Muster!* And the entire company assembled on the parade ground in battle order, the guns now hitched to horses, the cannonballs and powder loaded on wagons, the soldiers mounted and ready to ride out.

All except, of course, for the small detail of a dozen men and a corporal left behind to defend the fort. As Major Oliver Spoongurgle came slowly and reluctantly down the steps, his eye fell on them.

"Who are they?" he barked. "Why are they not mounted?"

"Defence detail, sir," replied Captain Sam Sutton.

"Rubbish!" cried the Major. "We need every man we can take. There might be more than one Indian. I'm not going into battle against odds like that, Captain!"

"Very well," said the Captain, for time was pressing and while they were standing arguing, Sitting Bull was on the move, "then we'll have to

take the cook-house detail and the boy with the goat. We can't possibly leave them to…"

"Are you out of your mind?" yelled the Major. "Mess up the whole look of the thing with those three misshapen louts and that midget and his walking doormat? Bugler, sound the advance!"

There was nothing further that the Captain could say. The Major was, after all, his superior officer. So, as the bugler blew, and the long blue column began to wind through the gates at a bridle-jingling trot, with the sun glinting off every piece of perfectly polished equipment and with the great cannon trundling along at the rear, five pairs of eyes were left behind to watch them go. Even Webster the goat seemed to sense that all was not as it should be, as the troops and horses and guns dwindled in the picture-frame of the gateway, leaving only their dust rising slowly on the morning air.

But if Private Conk and Private Bingle and Private Wibbley were trembling beneath their aprons at the dreadful thought of what might happen if the Indians realised that Fort Moccasin was utterly undefended, Arthur had no intention of letting such worries get the better of him.

"Right," he said, putting his hands on his hips and looking around him at the others, "the first thing we'd better do is shut the gate!"

"Very smart!" exclaimed Private Wibbley. "Very smart indeed!"

The other two Privates agreed, nodding vigorously. Arthur walked across to the long mirror, looked, and was forced to admit to himself that he did look pretty good in uniform; even if it was only Private Bingle's second-best uniform, cut down to Arthur's size, and Private Conk's second-best cap, with a pleat taken in at the back so that it sat very snugly on Arthur's head.

"Of course," said Arthur, "it'll only fool the enemy from a considerable distance. I'm a bit short for a US cavalryman."

"Oh, I wouldn't say that," said Private Bingle, who was secretly so delighted to be standing next to a soldier shorter than he was that he almost forgot the terrifying circumstances that had brought it about.

"Not that it matters much, anyhow," said Private Conk, somewhat gloomily, from his great height above them. "Even if we were all twice as big as I am, that still wouldn't put the enemy off. The Sioux aren't going to turn and run when they see just four soldiers."

"Nonsense!" cried Arthur, realizing that this was no time to be *too* polite. "Don't be a defeatist, Private Conk! It isn't how many we are that counts, it's what we can manage to do. Let's go outside and work out a Plan!"

So they marched out into the morning sunshine, and into the centre of the immaculate parade-ground; and there can be little doubt that if Major Oliver Spoongurgle had seen these four unmatching uniformed shapes scrunching across his precious gravel, he would have fallen down in a dead faint. But for Conk and Wibbley and Bingle, it was wonderful to be in cavalry blue again, and out of their aprons. Except, of course, for the one thing that was missing.

"If only," muttered Private Bingle, "we had rifles!"

"Or revolvers!" cried Conk.

"Or swords, even!" said Wibbley, slashing at the air with the soup-ladle he had brought along, just for something to carry as a weapon.

"Well," said Arthur, "the fact of the matter is that we must make the Indians, if they do attack, *think* we have guns. There wouldn't be any point in chucking potatoes at them or charging them with your broom-handle spears, even though that would be jolly brave, because that would get us nowhere at all, except dead. It would be worse then useless, in fact, because they'd realise immediately that they were the best weapons we had. No, the most important thing is to make the fort look full of soldiers: we'll have to light fires in all the fire-places, so that all the chimneys smoke, and we'll have to make as much noise as we can blowing bugles and banging pots and pans together, and we'll all have to run along the firing platforms,

poking our heads out at different places, so that it seems as though there are lots of soldiers, and we'll have to keep on shouting at one another, all that sort of thing."

"Poke our heads out?" enquired Private Conk nervously, thinking of the stories he had heard about Sioux marksmen who could shoot a pea off a post from half a mile away.

"Yes," replied Arthur firmly.

"It won't be any use," said Private Bingle. "As soon as they ride towards the fort, they'll realise that nobody is shooting at them, and that will be that."

"Ah," said Arthur, "I've thought about that. We may not have any guns, but we *do* have gunpowder. What we'll do is put little piles of it all along the firing platform, and if the enemy does attack, we'll run along with a burning torch and set them off. The bangs might discourage them."

Private Conk looked down at him.

"It's a good job you said *might*," he muttered. "I was beginning to think you were barmy."

"The trouble with you, Private Conk," said Arthur sternly, "is you give up too easily."

Private Conk sighed.

"The trouble with *me*," he replied, "is that I'm twice as big a target as anybody else. If you were me, Arthur, you'd worry, too."

The two other Privates went very pale at this, and even Webster the goat seemed to sense that the conversation had taken an unsettling turn, and stopped chewing. Arthur however, merely set his jaw more firmly.

"I don't think we ought to talk about targets," he said briskly. "There's work to be done."

And they began to do it.

The day went rather well, all things considered, and one of the best things about being busy was that the four friends had no time to stop and think about bullets, arrows, tomahawks, and all the rest of it.

They set the little piles of gunpowder according to Arthur's instructions, and they kept the fires stoked, and they set up a washing-line on the roof of the cook-house where it could be seen from outside the fort and give the impression, from the dozens of pairs of pants they hung on it, that the place was filled to overflowing with soldiers waiting for clean underwear; and they also managed to find a number of spare uniforms, which they buttoned up and stuffed with straw. On the collars of these they placed turnips, each turnip painted to look – from a distance – like a face, and they put caps on the turnips, and when this was done they

propped the dummies in the firing-gaps around the walls of the fort, so that the enemy would think the dummies were real live soldiers.

And when all the work was finished, and evening began to fall, and they realised they had managed to get through at least one day without an Indian

attack, they built a big fire in the middle of Major Oliver Spoongurgle's precious parade-ground, and the cooked their evening meal on it, because, as Arthur pointed out, if there *were* any Indian scouting parties about, it wouldn't hurt at all to let them see the smoke and flames of a large fire, and even smell the delicious smell of sizzling steaks and hear the crackle of baked potatoes as they jumped and popped in the bright yellow heart of the bonfire.

Because there would be no way for those Indians to tell that sitting around those roaring flames were just three kitchen-cleaners and a small boy of about seven. Not forgetting, of course, Webster the goat.

And when the meal was finished, they rolled themselves in their thick blue cavalry blankets beside the glowing fire, and, knowing that the Sioux would not attack at night, they slept.

They woke as dawn rolled back the darkness.

But it wasn't the silver light in the sky that woke them.

And it wasn't the sudden, sharp bite of the early cold.

And it wasn't the piercing cries of birds rising in the lightening sky.

It was something else.

Arthur, who was a very light sleeper, was the first to hear it. He rolled over, waking Webster the goat, who had been sleeping on his feet and dreaming of potato peel.

He stood up, his hand over Webster's muzzle to quieten him, and he listened hard.

There it was again!

A high, looping cry, not quite a coyote's cry, not quite a timber-wolf's howl, yet very like them.

He nudged Private Bingle, and when Bingle's eyes snapped open, Arthur put a finger to his friend's lips. Then he moved quickly across and woke the other two.

All four listened.

The strange whoop came again!

"What is it?" whispered Private Bingle.

"I can't be absolutely sure," replied Arthur, quietly and calmly, "but it could very well be Sioux scouts signalling to one another!"

"Oh, heavens!" muttered Private Wibbley.

"B-b-b-b-b-!" stammered Private Conk. "G-g-g-g-g-!"

But whatever it was he wanted to say, his chattering teeth would not allow anything else to get past them.

"You wait here," said Arthur, "and get ready for possible action. You all know what you have to do. I'm going up the ladder to the observation platform."

Whereupon he crossed the parade ground at a silent tip-toeing run, swung himself up onto the ladder, and began, very swiftly, to climb to the top.

When Arthur reached the observation platform, the landscape that spread out beneath him was so startlingly beautiful that he almost forgot his reason for being there: as the sun broke, golden, over the rim of mountains to the east, the light flowed across the broad sweep of valley, turning the Milk River to a ribbon of pale honey. Arthur thought he had never seen anything quite so peaceful in his entire life: it seemed quite unbelievable that down there, in the soft morning stillness and the gently rising mists, there was

a dangerous enemy, waiting its moment to pounce, shrieking and firing, upon Fort Moccasin.

He stared into this unmoving picture, peering through slitted eyes for some tiny sign which would give away the enemy's presence. Nothing stirred, save the odd tawny jack-rabbit bouncing across his green field like a furry ball, or a tree changing colour gently as the light breeze turned its leaves.

Perhaps they weren't there at all? Perhaps the whoop *had* been some mountain animal after all? Perhaps his imagination had…

And then he saw them.

A bush moved, a few hundred yards to the left of the fort, and two dark shapes stood there for a second before the bush folded them in again. And, to the right this time, he spotted three more. Sioux scouts, spying out the lie of the fort. And, as the light grew stronger, there, on the banks of the Milk River a couple of miles to the north, he could just distinguish a darkish mass that wasn't trees or bushes or anything else but a large force of men and horses.

Quickly, Arthur swung himself back onto the ladder and slid to the ground again. The other three looked at him, not daring to ask.

Arthur just nodded.

"I should think they're only waiting for the light to get full," he said quietly.

But for once Arthur was wrong.

Because, even as he said it, a far, faint rumble caught their ears; and this time those ears were in no doubt whatever.

"They're c-c-c-c-c-!" cried Private Conk, grabbing Private Bingle.

"Yes," muttered Private Wibbley, "they're coming, all right!"

"Right!" shouted Arthur, who had no intention of standing there trembling and stuttering. "Get to the firing platforms! Sound the bugles! Shout as loudly as you can!"

Not, Arthur thought, even as he ran himself, that shouting and bugling was going to do any good now. The Indians had scouted the fort, not been put off by signs of life or the dummies propped against the embrasures, and would probably have attacked even if the cavalry had still been there in full strength. Still, Arthur said to himself as he reached his position on the firing platform and lit his torch, you have to do what you can…

He glanced over the top of the wall, and gasped! That same view, so peaceful five minutes earlier, was now alive with charging, whooping men, bearing down in a great billowing line of horses that seemed to fill the landscape from end to end. The noise of the Privates' bugles was utterly washed away by the thunder and the shrieking of the Indian attack, and now, here and there along the line, Arthur noticed, with a cold clenching of his stomach, the puffs of smoke and stabs of flame that spat from the guns the Sioux were firing as they rode!

Beside him, a dummy flew backwards, the air filled with whirling straw from the terrible bullet, and slowly tumbled, broken, to the ground below.

"NOW!" yelled Arthur, though the others probably couldn't hear, and touched his torch to the little piles of gunpowder.

They did not really bang, for powder has to be

compressed into a gunbarrel before it will explode properly, but they went up in great WHOOSHES, and smoke and flame burst from twenty places along the wall, and the effect was really not too different from that of a line of cannon firing.

And, as luck would have it, the general noise and excitement of the charge was such that the Indians did not immediately notice that the thunder of guns was missing. They had, after all, been prepared for firing from the walls, and when they saw the smoke and flames leap up from the whole length of Fort Moccasin, they naturally reeled and reined and swerved, and the horses, startled by all this, lurched into one another, so that several riders were hurled to the ground; and other warriors, seeing this happen, automatically assumed that their companions had been struck by cannonballs or bullets, and they, too, were thrown into confusion, and broke stride, some pulling up, some bearing away to left and right, until at last the line was not a line at all but rather a ragged mess of men and horses in disconnected groups which had suddenly stopped going forward.

Whereupon three or four of the Sioux leaders whooped a special signal that was taken up from group to group, and the whole company of Indians wheeled about and began to gallop furiously back the way they had come.

On the ramparts, Arthur and his three grown-up friends, their faces blackened by powder-smoke, watched them go.

"Hurrah!" cried Private Conk, hardly believing his eyes. "We've beaten them off! Three cheers for Arthur!"

But Arthur shook his head.

"I'm afraid not," he said. "If there had only been a few of them, it might have worked. They might have calculated what they thought were the odds, and decided not to take the risk. But the Sioux are very brave, and extraordinarily tough, and right now their leaders are probably planning their next charge and reckoning that enough of them will get past our guns this time to smash down the gates, or swarm over the walls, and take the fort." Here Arthur gave a grim little smile. "And we know they'll get past our guns without much trouble, don't we?"

The happy relief had drained out of his friends' faces while Arthur had been talking. But they were soldiers, still; so Private Wibbley set his jaw and said:

"Right, lads, then it's up and at 'em with potatoes and forks!"

Arthur looked at him, feeling very proud that Private Wibbley was his friend. But what he said was:

"It's just possible it may not come to that."

They stared at him.

"I have," said Arthur, "an Emergency Plan. I didn't mention it before, because I didn't want anyone to start worrying that we might *need* an Emergency Plan. But it looks very much as though we do, and I'm going to try it."

"What is it?" cried Private Conk, desperately, and thinking that anything was better than facing several hundred Sioux warriors armed only with a potato. "What shall we do?"

"Not you," replied Arthur, glacing quickly through a firing-slot to make sure the Sioux hadn't yet turned to begin their second charge. "The Plan is just for me and Webster!"

Hearing his name, Webster, who had been waiting patiently in the parade-ground, pricked up his shaggy ears. But they weren't pricked anywhere

near as high as Private Bingle's!

"*You and Webster*?" he exclaimed. "What on earth…?"

"We'll need a white flag of truce," said Arthur calmly, "and you three will have to pull the gate open for me."

"You're going," whispered Private Conk hoarsely, "out *there*?"

"I'm going," replied Arthur, "to talk to the Indians!"

One minute later, as the three Privates stared in terror from the open gates of Fort Moccasin, Arthur William Foskett and Webster the goat walked slowly into the sun towards the point where the Sioux were preparing to re-start their attack.

Arthur was carrying a white pillow-case tied to a broom-handle, and his heart, for all his amazing bravery, was beating in his ears with the clatter of a tin drum.

As Arthur approached, a brave clutched the arm of the Sioux chief beside him, and pointed.

The chief stared!

It was a tiny cavalryman and a goat. What did it mean? Why did this peculiar couple come towards him under a white flag of truce?

But as he was an experienced warrior who ignored nothing just because it seemed extraordinary, and as he always respected a flag of truce, he nudged his pony with his knees, and slowly went forward, with three or four of his braves, to meet Arthur and Webster.

Now, Arthur, for all his many talents and skills, did not speak the Sioux language; but he reckoned that a great Sioux chief with hundreds of warriors under his command who had been fighting the army for many years would probably speak a little English.

So it proved.

The small group of warriors stopped. Arthur and Webster stopped. They faced one another for a few moments, silently. Then Arthur put up his right hand, this being the sign the Indians used to show they did not carry a weapon and came only to talk, and said:

"Good morning."

The chief put up his hand, and said:

"How" and then "Good morning, mister."

And then Webster the goat got up on his two hind legs, and said:

"Good morning, O great and mighty chief of the Sioux!"

Well, you can just imagine what effect *that* had on the Indians! Their horses reared up in astonishment, of course, but they weren't half as astonished as their riders, I can tell you! In fact, the braves who accompanied the chief cried out, and leapt from their horses, and fell to their knees on the ground in front of Webster.

For the Sioux were a people of many deep and, to us, strange beliefs, and many peculiar superstitions; and perhaps the most important among these was that their gods inhabited strange forms, and could

speak to them in the wind and in the water and in the thunder; and what was more natural than to believe, when you heard a goat on its hind legs speak, that a god had chosen this form to address you?

But the chief did not dismount, for he *was* a chief, and for his people's sake was cautious in what he said and did. Although, of course, he was deeply shaken by Webster; he stared at him from eyes wide and white beneath the orange war-paint of their lids, and when he spoke, his voice was low and shaky.

"Do you speak to me, Chief Cloud-That-Dances of the mighty Sioux people? Or is it the wind that plays tricks in my ears?"

Webster did a little circular walk before replying.
"O bravest of the brave, Chief Cloud-That-Dances," said Webster, in a deep and thrilling voice, "to whom should I speak, I who am Walking Goat, messenger of the gods, if not to you, the great leader of his people?"
Chief Cloud-That-Dances slowly dismounted at this. He raised his great head to the sky and shook his rifle high above it, and called out, in his own language:
"IT IS TRUE! THE GOD-GOAT TALKS!"
And the warriors behind him, hearing his shout, set up the same great echoing cry:

"THE GOD-GOAT TALKS! THE GOD-GOAT TALKS TO CLOUD-THAT-DANCES!"

The chief lowered his rifle, and murmured to Webster:

"What message do you bring me, O great Walking Goat?"

"I have lived with the pony-soldiers," replied Webster, "and I know they do not want this war with the Sioux nation. This is also the wish of the gods, who ask Chief Cloud-That-Dances to return in peace to his people and settle his arguments with the white man without the spilling of blood."

Chief Cloud-That-Dances nodded gravely.

"I shall heed the advice of the gods, O great Walking Goat," he said; and he beckoned his kneeling braves to rise and remount, and slowly the little group rode back to the waiting Sioux army,

and slowly, too, that army in its turn wheeled its horses' heads round to face north again, and began to move back across the Milk River.

Leaving Arthur and Webster standing alone, watching them go. Until, finally, they too turned and, with Webster once more on all fours, walked back across the green plain to Fort Moccasin.

When Major Oliver Spoongurgle rode into Fort Moccasin at the head of his company on the following day, he was a very different man from the one who had ridden out two days before.

True, the first order he gave was for everyone to go in *immediately* and have a bath and put on clean uniforms and shave and splash their faces with lavender-water, so he wasn't *that* different, but the main point was that he was smiling, and joking, and slapping people on the back, and when I tell you that three of those people were Privates Bingle, Wibbley and Conk, you'll understand how great a change had come over Major Oliver Spoongurgle.

And the reason for this was not only that the war was over – something, it must be said, which the Major had learned the evening before from a special messenger who had had great difficulty in catching up with the Spoongurgle company, so fast had it been riding in the *opposite* direction from the enemy – but that it was over because of a peace

which Chief Cloud-That-Dances had made with the garrison at Fort Moccasin. When the messenger had told him the news, the Major had felt there had been some mistake, since he couldn't for the life of him remember that there was a garrison at Fort Moccasin.

But, bit by bit, the story of the small boy who could throw his voice and the goat who could walk on two legs and the three cook-house cleaners who had held off an Indian attack with puffs of smoke pieced itself together until Major Oliver Spoongurgle was beside himself with delight at all

the congratulations that poured in from other companies and other forts, telling him what a splendid leader he must be to have such brilliant and daring men and goats under his command!

And when word leaked out to him as he was riding back to the fort in the morning, that there was A Very Strong Possibility that he would be made a colonel for this, Major Oliver Spoongurgle nearly fell off his horse for joy, already seeing himself in his gorgeous colonel's uniform at the head of an entire regiment of impeccably marching men!

Which was why, as soon as he had shaved and dressed, he summoned the five heroes, including Webster the goat, to his quarters.

"Wonderful!" shouted the Major, beaming at them. "Splendid! What a fine body of men!"

They didn't know quite what to say to this, since they were all, as you know, modest fellows, and certainly not at all used to Spoongurgle compliments. So none of them said anything, except poor Private Conk, who was so embarrassed he could only murmur:

"I'm sorry I'm so tall, sir."

To which Major Oliver Spoongurgle immediately replied:

"Nonsense, Conk! You're the perfect height for your size! I've always said so, haven't I, Captain?"

Captain Sam Sutton cleared his throat and looked at the ceiling.

"And as for that goat," continued the Major cheerily, "as soon as I set eyes on him, I knew he was just the goat for us! What bearing! What style!"

"Thank you," said Webster.

The Major threw back his head and roared with laughter.

"Arthur my boy, you must be the best ventriloquist in all the world!" he shouted.

"Oh, it's very easy, really," said Arthur.

"Rubbish!" retorted the Major. His face grew thoughtful. "Of course, we'll have to get you your own uniform. Can't have you leading Webster about in Bingle's old jacket, can we?"

"Leading Webster?" said Arthur. "Oh, I'm afraid I shan't be able to stay. I have to go home this afternoon. They're expecting me."

They all looked at him, suddenly silent and suddenly sad.

"I was forgetting," murmured Major Oliver Spoongurgle. "You turned out to be such a splendid soldier, I'd quite forgotten you weren't really in the cavalry at all."

"He *was*, though," said Captain Sam Sutton, quietly. "If only for a couple of days. And very lucky the cavalry was to have him, too!"

"Hear, hear!" cried the Major. "It just goes to

show that appearances aren't everything, I suppose."

The others gazed at him in amazement. Major Oliver Spoongurgle was a changed man all right, of that there was no doubt at all! As for the Major himself, he stood up, saluted Arthur smartly, and shook his hand.

"You'll come back and see us, though," he said, "won't you?"

"Oh, yes," said Webster the goat, "he'll certainly do that!"